TOP 10 SCARIEST ANIMALS

Children's Press®
An imprint of Scholastic Inc.

BY BRENNA MALONEY

A special thank-you to the team at the Cincinnati Zoo & Botanical Garden for their expert consultation.

Library of Congress Cataloging-in-Publication Data available

ISBN 978-1-5461-3608-8 (library binding)
ISBN 978-1-5461-3609-5 (paperback)

10 9 8 7 6 5 4 3 25 26 27 28 29

Printed in China 62
First edition, 2025

Book design by Kay Petronio

FANGTOOTH FISH

WOLVERINE FROG

CONTENTS

THE WORLD OF SCARY

FANGTOOTH FISH

GOLIATH BIRDEATER

GOBLIN SHARK

ASIAN GIANT HORNET

There are so many scary animals in our wild world! Some of these animals look spooky. Some have big teeth. Some have sharp claws.

Some do frightening things. They bite. They sting! But . . . are you ready to discover which one is the absolute scariest? Read on and count down from ten to one to learn which animal takes the top spot!

MOZAMBIQUE SPITTING COBRA

SARCASTIC FRINGEHEAD

HAMMER-HEADED BAT

CASSOWARY

WOLVERINE FROG

TASMANIAN DEVIL

#10 FANGTOOTH FISH

FIERCE!

FACT FILE

ANIMAL GROUP: Fish

HABITAT: Oceans

AVERAGE SIZE: A smartphone

DIET: Carnivore

This spooky creature lives deep down in the ocean. Finding a meal in the dark is not easy. But this **predator** is a powerful hunter. It stabs its **prey** with giant fangs. Then it swallows its meal whole.

A fangtooth can eat fish one-third its size. It may seem like a big monster. But it is tiny! The average fangtooth is only 6 inches (15 cm) long.

FACT For their body size, fangtooths have some of the largest teeth of any ocean animal.

FANGTOOTH FISH CLOSE-UP

BODY

Its body is covered with prickly scales and spines.

TAIL

A powerful tail helps it chase after prey.

FACT

The fangtooth fish is also called the ogre fish. "Ogre" means monster!

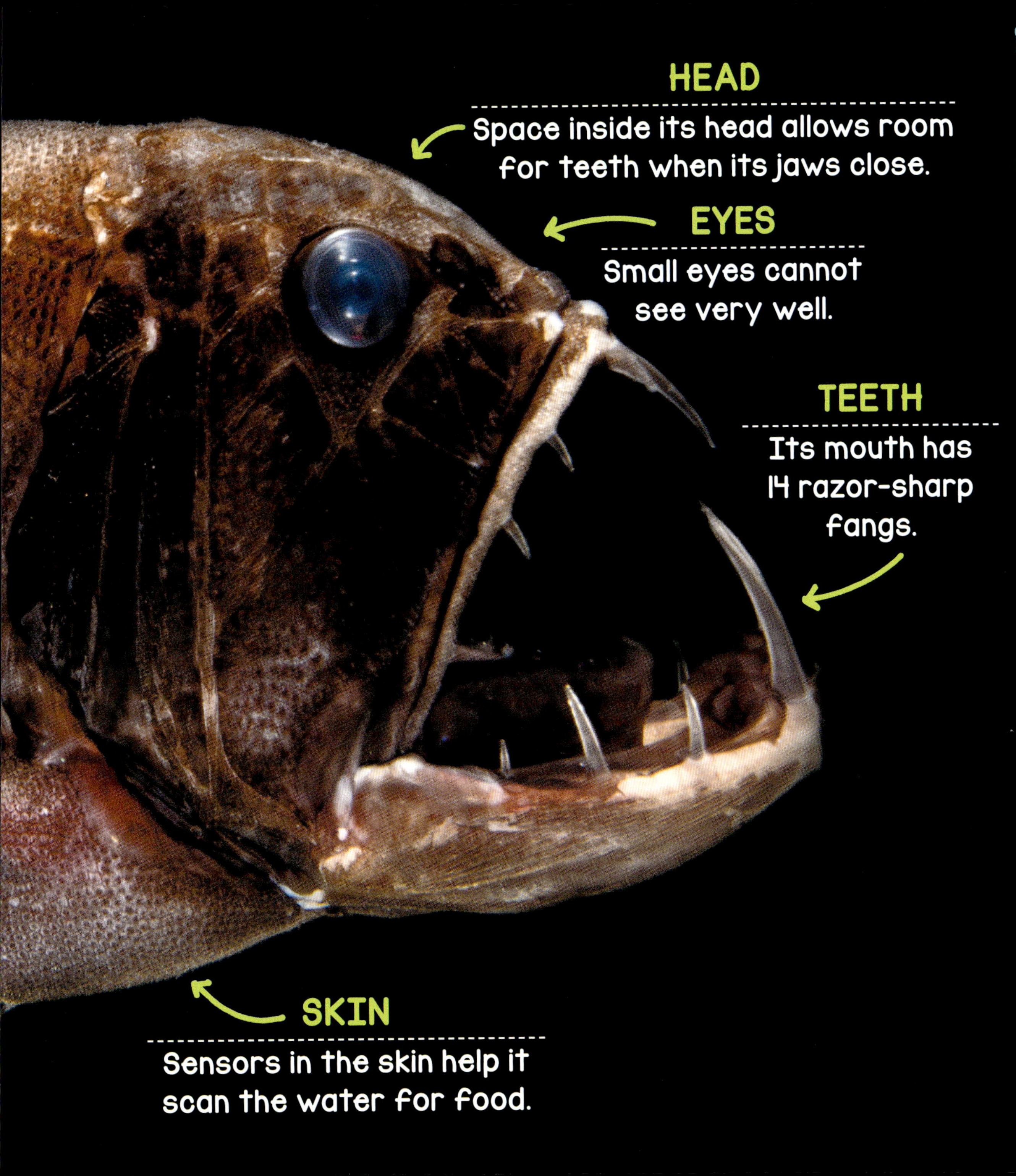
HEAD
Space inside its head allows room for teeth when its jaws close.
EYES
Small eyes cannot see very well.
TEETH
Its mouth has 14 razor-sharp fangs.
SKIN
Sensors in the skin help it scan the water for food.

#9 HAMMER-HEADED BAT

LOUD!

FACT FILE

ANIMAL GROUP: Mammal

HABITAT: Forests

AVERAGE SIZE: A sheet of paper

DIET: Herbivore

The hammer-headed bat is one of the largest bats in the world. Males have a wingspan of up to 3 feet (1 m) across. That's as long as a baseball bat. It has bulging eyes. Its face is fleshy.

FACT
This mammal is also called a big-lipped bat.

Wait until you hear its hair-raising honking! Males have a large voice box to call out loudly to other bats. This creature might give you the creeps. But it is a harmless fruit-slurper. That big nose sniffs out figs, bananas, and mangoes.

#8 GOBLIN SHARK

SAVAGE!

FACT FILE

ANIMAL GROUP: Fish

HABITAT: Oceans

AVERAGE SIZE: A compact car

DIET: Carnivore

It is easy to be afraid of a big animal that lives in the dark. Seeing a goblin shark might give you the shivers! It has pinkish, see-through skin. Its long, flat snout looks like a blade. It has sharp, nail-like teeth.

A goblin shark can launch its entire jaw out from its head! That is how the shark catches prey. Its sharp teeth clamp down hard. Prey is sucked into the shark's mouth within seconds.

FACT These sharks have lived on Earth for millions of years.

#7 GOLIATH BIRDEATER

VENOMOUS!

FACT FILE

ANIMAL GROUP: Invertebrate

HABITAT: Rainforests

AVERAGE SIZE: A dinner plate

DIET: Carnivore

This tarantula is the largest spider on Earth. Does it really eat birds? Sometimes! More often it eats insects, frogs, and rodents. The giant spider sinks its inch-long fangs into its prey.

FACT Female Goliath birdeaters can live for up to 25 years.

Then it drags the dying animal back to its **burrow**. The **venom** in its bite turns the prey's insides into liquid. Then the Goliath birdeater drinks its dinner. It can also shoot stinging hairs from its body to stun predators.

#6 SARCASTIC FRINGEHEAD

SNEAKY!

FACT FILE

ANIMAL GROUP: Fish

HABITAT: Oceans

AVERAGE SIZE: An adult male hand

DIET: **Omnivore**

It is hard to spot a sarcastic fringehead. It is usually hidden in its ocean-floor **den**. Then it darts forward with its mouth open. This fish fights off anything it thinks is a threat.

As it lunges forward, its mouth opens even wider. The skin flaps on its head flare out. Then this fish sticks out its black tongue. Its sharp, needle-like teeth pierce small shellfish that come too close.

FACT These fish get their name from the soft frills on the tops of their heads.

#5 CASSOWARY

AGGRESSIVE!

FACT FILE

ANIMAL GROUP: Bird

HABITAT: Forests

AVERAGE SIZE: A surfboard

DIET: Omnivore

Stay away! The world's most dangerous bird wants to be left alone. Cassowaries are shy, **solitary** animals. They hiss in warning. If threatened, a cassowary will kick and claw.

It can jump almost as high as it is tall into the air. A cassowary's middle toes have 4-inch (10-cm) dagger-like claws. This bird can slice any threat with one swift kick.

FACT

A cassowary can run up to 31 miles per hour (50 kph). That is faster than any human!

#4 ASIAN GIANT HORNET

STINGING!

FACT FILE

ANIMAL GROUP: Invertebrate

HABITAT: Forests

AVERAGE SIZE: A double-A battery

DIET: Omnivore

Watch out! You do *not* want to meet an Asian giant hornet. It is the largest hornet in the world. It eats other insects. This hornet snips off the head of its prey. Then, it feeds the prey's body to its young.

Normally, hornets hunt alone. But *these* hornets work together to take on large prey. Asian giant hornets also sting. It feels like hot metal burning into the skin.

FACT This insect is also called the murder hornet.

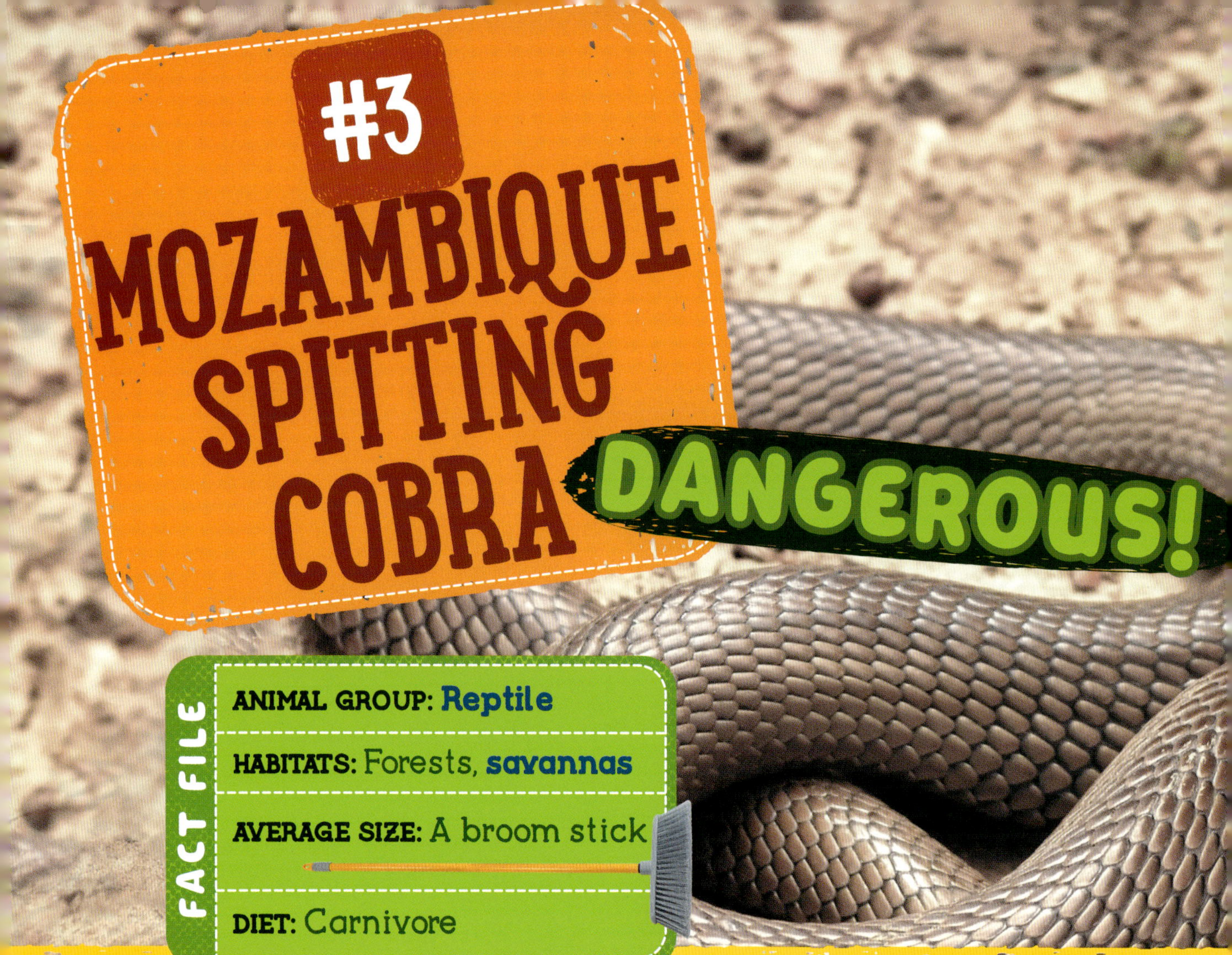

#3 MOZAMBIQUE SPITTING COBRA

DANGEROUS!

FACT FILE

ANIMAL GROUP: Reptile

HABITATS: Forests, savannas

AVERAGE SIZE: A broom stick

DIET: Carnivore

This snake is not just scary. It is also fierce! Come too close and it will spit venom in your eyes. When threatened, this snake raises its body off the ground. It flattens and widens its neck to form a hood.

FACT This cobra can climb trees and bushes. It is also an excellent swimmer.

The snake throws its mouth open. It can spray venom as far away as 6.5 feet (2 m)! That's about as long as a twin mattress. The venom causes pain, swelling, blisters—even blindness. It is one of the most dangerous snakes in Africa!

#2 TASMANIAN DEVIL

VICIOUS!

FACT FILE

ANIMAL GROUP: Mammal

HABITATS: Forests, woodlands

AVERAGE SIZE: A skateboard

DIET: Carnivore

Its high-pitched scream will make your blood run cold. The feisty Tasmanian devil is known for its eerie sounds. It growls, snarls, barks, and screeches as it hunts for food. It mostly eats smaller mammals.

This scary beast can be combative. It bares its teeth and lunges at threats. It devours prey quickly and leaves nothing behind. The devil's head, neck, and jaws are well-suited for crushing bones.

FACT

The Tasmanian devil has one of the most powerful bites of any mammal!

#1 TERRIFYING!

WOLVERINE FROG

FACT FILE

ANIMAL GROUP: **Amphibian**

HABITAT: Lowland forests

AVERAGE SIZE: A toilet paper roll

DIET: Carnivore

Be afraid. Be very afraid! The scariest animal is the wolverine frog. It is also called the hairy frog. When threatened, this frog does something terrifying.

The frog squeezes its muscles to break the bones in its toes. The bones burst through its skin. They form sharp "claws" for fighting. After using its claws, they go back inside. The skin and bones heal.

FACT

Wolverine frogs make scary noises, too. Their calls sound like a creaky door!

EYES

Its eyeballs help push food down its throat.

TEETH

A wide mouth holds several rows of teeth.

VOICE

This frog makes low sounds that can be felt by other frogs.

HANDS

Food is swallowed whole with help from its long fingers.

FACT

The wolverine frog is also called the horror frog. "Horror" means frightening!

WOLVERINE FROG CLOSE-UP

SKIN

Hair-like strands of skin on males help them breathe better.

X-ray of toe bones

CLAWS

Temporary "claws" can form from the frog's toe bones.

SIZING THEM UP

There are so many scary animals in our wild world! They bite. They sting. They spit. They have big teeth. They have sharp claws. Do you agree that the wolverine frog is the scariest? Or would you pick a different animal? You can probably find even more scary animals and make your own list!

GLOSSARY

amphibian (am-FIB-ee-uhn) a cold-blooded animal with a backbone that lives in water and breathes with gills when young

burrow (BUR-oh) a tunnel or hole in the ground made or used as a home by an animal

carnivore (KAHR-nuh-vor) an animal that eats meat

den the home of an animal

herbivore (HUR-buh-vor) an animal that only eats plants

invertebrate (in-VUR-tuh-brit) an animal without a backbone

mammal (MAM-uhl) a warm-blooded animal that has hair or fur and usually gives birth to live babies

omnivore (AHM-nuh-vor) an animal that eats both plants and meat

predator (PRED-uh-tur) an animal that lives by hunting other animals for food

prey (pray) an animal that is hunted by another animal for food

reptile (REP-tile) a cold-blooded animal that crawls across the ground or creeps on short legs; most have backbones and reproduce by laying eggs

savanna (suh-VAN-uh) a flat, grassy plain with few or no trees

solitary (SAH-li-ter-ee) single or only

venom (VEN-uhm) poison produced by some snakes and spiders that can pass to a victim through a bite or sting

INDEX

Page numbers in **bold** indicate images.

ABOUT THE AUTHOR

Brenna Maloney is the author of many books. She lives in Washington, DC, with her husband and two sons. She thinks the animals in this book are more cool than scary!